For Lucy and Jessica Andrews

A Red Fox Book

Published by Random House Children's Books
20 Vauxhall Bridge Road, London SW1V 2SA

A division of Random House UK Ltd
London Melbourne Sydney Auckland
Johannesburg and agencies throughout the world

1 3 5 7 9 10 8 6 4 2

First published in Great Britain by Hutchinson Children's Books 1992

Red Fox edition 1994

Printed in Singapore

RANDOM HOUSE UK Limited Reg. No. 954009

Starring Fred and Ursulina

Suzy-Jane Tanner

RED FOX

Ursulina and Fred had just started school. On their first morning,
Mrs Mishka the teacher called the register.
'Frederika Brown?' she enquired.
Fred pretended not to hear.
She never answered to her real name.

Ursulina liked music and movement.

Fred preferred nature study.

What both twins liked best of all was when Mrs Mishka couldn't tell them apart.

Not that this ever lasted very long.
Whatever mess there was always landed on Fred. Ursulina never
seemed to get dirty.

One day, the headmaster came to tell the class that they would be putting on a show for the mums and dads. It was to be *Sleeping Beauty* and everyone would have a part.

The whole class auditioned to see which part suited them best.
Jason Kodiak, the class heart-throb, was to play Prince Charming.

Ursulina was chosen to star as Sleeping Beauty, who would be
kissed by Prince Charming at the end of the show.
Fred was chosen for the back end of Daisybelle the cow.

'I'm the star,' Ursulina told Mum when they got home.

Daisybelle didn't have any lines so Fred helped Ursulina learn her words.

Mum and Dad spent ages making the costumes.

Ursulina stood nice and still while Mum fitted hers. It had long dangly sleeves and a pointed hat. Fred's costume was made from a cut down pair of Dad's old trousers.

She wriggled so much that Mum stuck a pin into her by mistake. 'Ouch!'

Ursulina was so excited about the show that she refused to take her costume off at bedtime. She was especially thrilled about kissing Jason Kodiak. Fred could only moo in disgust. She thought Jason was a drip.

At last it was the morning of the show.
Ursulina decided to have one last practice on the way to the car.
She was just showing off her best twirl when she stepped backwards
onto Fred's skateboard.

The doctor at the hospital had to put Ursulina's broken leg in a plaster cast.
Fred wanted a plaster too.

Mum took the twins to school.
She explained that Ursulina couldn't be Sleeping Beauty with a broken leg.
Poor Ursulina was extra upset because she wouldn't get to kiss Jason.
'Whatever shall we do?' wondered Mrs Mishka.

Mum pointed out that Fred knew Ursulina's part. The costume would fit too.
'Hail Princess Fred!' announced Mrs Mishka.
'Yuk,' said Fred.

Fred didn't want to be Sleeping Beauty and she certainly didn't want to kiss Jason Kodiak!

First she refused point-blank.
Then she stamped her foot and threw her very best tantrum.
Nobody took any notice.

Fred almost managed to sneak away, but she was spotted.
'What about Daisybelle?' she asked hopefully.
'Someone else can play Daisybelle,' answered Mrs Mishka.
'The show must go on!'

It took some time for Mum and Mrs Mishka to force Fred into her costume.
Mrs Mishka kept an eye on her until the show started.
'But it's not fair!' wailed Fred.

Lots of mums and dads arrived to watch the show.

Ursulina sat in the wings in case Fred forgot her lines. Fred remembered all the words but she kept getting tangled in her dangly sleeves.

Fred got a bit bored waiting to prick her finger on the magic spindle.
Nearly everyone laughed when she showed her knickers.

Sleeping Beauty was supposed to go to sleep for a hundred years.
But Fred just couldn't keep still that long.
She wriggled around and made faces at Ursulina.

Then it was time for Prince Charming to awaken her with a kiss.
It was too much.
Fred smacked Jason Kodiak's face.

Jason smacked Fred back.

'Stop that!' shouted Ursulina from the wings, but they ignored her.

Fred was beginning to enjoy herself.

Mrs Mishka sent the flower fairies on stage to try to hide the fight.

The headmaster sent Daisybelle on from the other side to do the same.

Unfortunately, Daisybelle's new back end got out of step with the front. There was a great crash.

Jason Kodiak passed out cold. Ursulina hopped to his side.
'Speak to me Jason!' she begged. Then she kissed him.

Jason opened his eyes and grinned. He had only been pretending!

So Ursulina got her kiss after all. Everyone else got several plasters which made them feel better.

Then they took it in turns to bow to the audience. Fred and Ursulina got the loudest cheers and the most laughs. Mum couldn't be cross with Fred for long.

'The show starred Fred *and* Ursulina after all,' she said.